SAMANTHA
SCHOLTZ

S

THE USBORNE PICTURE DICTIONARY

Felicity Brooks

Designer and modelmaker: Jo Litchfield

Design and additional illustrations by
Mike Olley and Brian Voakes

Photography by Howard Allman

Contents

2 Using your dictionary
5 The dictionary
90 Colors and shapes
91 Numbers
92 Days and months
93 The seasons
94 Family words
95 Words we use a lot

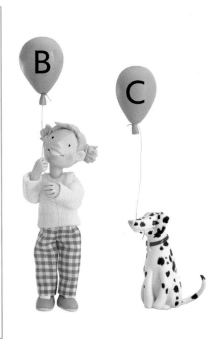

Managing Designer: Mary Cartwright
Americanization Editor: Carrie Seay
Editorial Assistant: Fiona Patchett

Additional models by Les Pickstock, Barry Jones, Stef Lumley, Karen Krige and Stefan Barnett

With thanks to Staedtler for providing the Fimo® material for models.
Bruder® toys supplied by Euro Toys and Models Ltd.

Using your dictionary

The words in a dictionary are in the same order as the letters of the alphabet. This means words that begin with A come first, then words that begin with B, and so on. In this dictionary there are many things on each page to help you to find the word you are looking for.

This letter in a blue square shows the first letter of the words on that page.

This word shows the first word on the page.

This word shows the last word on the page.

The words that you can look up are shown in blue. You can find out about the words in parentheses on page 4.

Don't forget that in a dictionary you read down the page in columns. In most other books you read across.

Sometimes the same word appears twice with little numbers next to it. This shows that the same word can be used in two very different ways.

If you forget the order of the letters in the alphabet, look at the bottom of any page.

The blue letter also shows the first letter of the words on that page.

S start *to* stool

start
do the first part of something; begin

The birds are starting to eat the seeds.

station
a place where people get on or off trains

stay
1. not leave a place

The cows stay in the field all day.

2. live with someone for a short time

steep
If a hill is steep, it slopes a lot and is hard to climb.

stick[1]
a long, thin piece of wood

stick[2] (stuck, stuck)
use glue to join something onto something else

still[1]
If someone or something is still, they are not moving at all.

Milo is standing very still.

still[2]
If something is still happening or is still there, it has not stopped or gone

Oliver ate one apple...

...but he still has some left.

sting (stung, stung)
If an animal or plant stings you, it pricks you and leaves some poison in your body.

Flora is afraid the bee will sting her.

stir
move something around with a spoon or stick

stone
a small rock

stool
a seat without a back

a b c d e f g h i j k l m n o p q r s t u v w x y z

How to find a word

1 Think of the letter the word starts with. "Stone" starts with an "s", for example.

2 Look through the dictionary until you have found the "s" pages.

3 Think of the next letter of the word. Look for words that begin with "st".

4 Now look at all the "st" words until you find your word.

Can you find?

For practice, you could try looking up these words:

bat

street

lion

hill

wash

jacket

cake

music

Alphabet game

Can you put the names of these fruits in alphabetical order?*

strawberry

lemon

cherry

raspberry

grapes

pineapple

apple

banana

*Answer: apple, banana, cherry, grapes, lemon, pineapple, raspberry, strawberry

Looking at a word

When you have looked up a word, here are some of the things you can find out.

You can find out what a word means.

hippopotamus
(also called a hippo)
a very big animal with short legs and thick skin

You can also find out if a word can be shortened.

You can find out how to spell a word.

know (knew, known)
1. If you know someone, you have met them before.

These children know each other.

2. have something in your mind

You can see how you can use a word.

You can see if a word can mean different things.

A picture tells you more about a word.

hen (also called a chicken)
a bird that farmers keep

This tells you another word for the same thing.

Net²
a short name for the Internet

You can find out if a word is short for something.

know (knew, known)
1. If you know someone, you have met them before.

Turn the page to find out about words in parentheses.

3

Talking about the past

"Doing" words, such as "walk", "smile" and "eat" are called verbs. When you use a verb to talk about the past (the time before now), you usually just add "ed" or "d" to the end of the word:

Danny likes to walk to school.

Yesterday Danny walked to school.

Danny has walked to school every day this week.

My baby can smile.

She smiled yesterday.

My baby has smiled a lot this week.

For some verbs, you don't add "d" or "ed", but another ending to talk about the past. Some verbs change completely:

Robert likes to **eat** pasta.

Yesterday he **ate** pasta.

He has **eaten** pasta every day this week.

In this dictionary, you can see these changes in parentheses ( ) after the word:

eat (ate, eaten)

Comparing words

"Describing" words, such as "small", "expensive" and "good" are called adjectives. When you use an adjective to compare things, you usually just add "er" or "est" to the end of the word:

A horse is small**er** than an elephant, but a mouse is the small**est**.

For some adjectives, instead of adding "er" or "est", you say "more" or "most" before the word:

A car is **more** expensive than a bicycle.

A truck is the **most** expensive.

You must be **more** careful.

Sara is the **most** careful.

For a very few adjectives, you don't add "er" or "est", or "more" or "most", but change the whole word:

This cake is **good**.

This cake is **better**.

This cake is the **best**.

In this dictionary, you can see these unusual words in parentheses ( ) after the word:

good (better, best)

More than one

"Naming" words, such as "goat", "sheep", "mouse" and "child" are called nouns. When you use a noun to talk about more than one thing, you usually add an "s" to the end of the word:

one goat   two goat**s**

one house   two house**s**

If the word already ends with an "s", you add "es" to the end instead:

one cross   two cross**es**

For a very few nouns, you don't add an "s" or "es" to the end, but keep the word exactly the same:

one sheep   two **sheep**

For a few nouns you add a completely different ending:

one child   two child**ren**

For some nouns, you don't change the ending, but you change the whole word:

one mouse   two **mice**

one goose   two **geese**

In this dictionary, you can see these unusual words in parentheses ( ) after the word:

child (children)

actor

someone who pretends to be another person and acts in a play

afraid

If you are afraid, you think something is scary or bad.

Maddy is afraid of spiders.

air

what we all breathe

A balloon floats in the air.

add

1. find the answer to a sum like this one:

$$8 + 2 =$$

2. put something with something else

Billy's adding two blocks.

after

If something happens after something else, it happens later.

Sacha goes after Suki.

Sacha

Suki

alone

not with other people

Katie's alone in the bathtub.

address

words that show where someone lives

Oliver Muncher
233 Grub Avenue
Tulsa OK 74146

afternoon

the part of the day after the morning

3 o'clock in the afternoon

alphabet

all the letters you use to write words, put in a special order:

abcdefghijklm
nopqrstuvwxyz

adult

a grown-up person

Minnie's dad is an adult.

age

how old you are

Olivia

Joshua

Ben

Can you guess Olivia's age?

ambulance

a special van that takes sick people to the hospital

a b c d e f g h i j k l m n o p q r s t u v w x y z

amount

how much there
is of something

a large
amount of
pasta

ankle

the part of your body that
joins your leg to your foot

ankle

apple

a round fruit with red, green
or yellow skin

angel

a messenger sent from
heaven

answer

what you say or write when
someone asks you a question

Question: Which animal says
                     "meow"?

Answer: A cat

arm

the part of your body
between your shoulder
and hand

angry

If you are angry, you feel
upset and want to shout.

ant

a very small insect

arrive

get to where you are going

The bus has just arrived.

animal

something that lives, moves
and breathes

ape

a large animal with long
arms and no tail

An orangutan is an ape.

art

something such as a painting
or drawing, that someone
has made

a b c d e f g h i j k l m n o p q r s t u v w x y z

Bb baby *to* balance

artist
someone who draws or paints or makes other pieces of art

ask
1. say that you want to know something

2. say that you want something

She is asking for strawberries.

asleep
sleeping

astronaut
someone who goes into space

baby
a very young child

back¹
the part of your body between your neck and bottom

back²
the part farthest from the front of something

This boy is sitting at the back of the bus.

bad (worse, worst)
1. naughty

a bad dog

2. not good or not good to eat

a bad apple

bag
something you use to hold or carry things

bake
cook food, such as bread or cake, in an oven

Oliver is going to bake some muffins.

baker
someone who makes and sells bread and cakes

balance
keep your body or something steady so it does not fall

This clown can balance on one hand.

a b c d e f g h i j k l m n o p q r s t u v w x y z

bald
Someone who is bald has no hair on his head.

ball
1. a round thing that you use for games

2. a big party where people dance

ballerina
a woman who does a kind of dancing called ballet

balloon
a thin, rubber bag that gets bigger when you blow into it

banana
a long, curved fruit with a yellow skin

band
a group of people who play music together

bang
a sudden, loud noise

bank
1. a place where people keep money safe

2. the edge of a river or stream

bar
1. a long, thin piece of metal or wood

2. a block of something

a bar of soap

bare
If you are bare, you have no clothes on.

bark[1]
the hard skin that covers a tree trunk

This log has rough, brown bark.

bark[2]
When a dog barks, it makes a loud noise in its throat.

Woof woof!

a b c d e f g h i j k l m n o p q r s t u v w x y z

barn
a large farm building for animals, straw or machines

base
the bottom part of something

a lamp with a yellow base

basket
something you use to hold or carry things

bat
1. a small, furry animal with wings

2. a kind of stick that you use to hit a ball

bathtub
something you fill with water and sit in to wash yourself

beach
land by the sea with sand or stones on it

playing on the beach

beak
the hard outside part of a bird's mouth

Toucans have big beaks.

bean
a long, thin vegetable, or the seeds inside it

bear
a big, wild animal with thick fur

beard
the hair on a man's chin

beautiful
very nice to look at, listen to or smell

a beautiful cake

bed
something you lie on to sleep or rest

a b c d e f g h i j k l m n o p q r s t u v w x y z

bedroom
a room you sleep in

before
If something happens before something else, it happens first.

Suki goes before Sacha.

Sacha

Suki

below
Something that is below something else is under it or lower than it.

The kitten is below the wood.

bee
a yellow and black insect that can fly. Some bees make honey.

begin (began, begun)
start to do something

Sam began to yawn.

belt
a long strip of plastic, leather or cloth that you wear around your tummy

beetle
a shiny insect with hard outside wings

behind
Something that is behind something else is at the back of it.

The kitten is behind the flowerpot.

beside
Something that is beside something else is next to it.

The kitten is beside the flowerpot.

beetroot (beetroot)
a round, dark red vegetable

belong
Something that belongs to you is yours.

The book belongs to Suzie.

between
Something that is between two things is in the middle of them.

The kitten is between the flowerpots.

a b c d e f g h i j k l m n o p q r s t u v w x y z

bib *to* book

bib
something that a baby wears around its neck to keep its clothes clean

birthday
the date that you were born

a birthday party

boat
something that floats and can carry people and things across water

bicycle
a machine with two wheels, that you can ride

bite (bit, bitten)
use your teeth to cut into something

body
Your body is every part of you.

— arm

— tummy

some parts of the body

— leg

— foot

big
large; not small

a big elephant

blanket
a thick cover that you can put on a bed

bone
the hard, white parts inside your body or inside an animal's body

Patch is gnawing a toy bone.

bird
an animal that has a beak, wings and feathers

blow (blew, blown)
1. make air come out of your mouth

2. When the wind blows, it moves the air.

book
something that you read that has pages attached inside a cover

a b c d e f g h i j k l m n o p q r s t u v w x y z

b boot *to* breakfast

boot
a tall shoe that covers your foot and ankle

bowl
a kind of round, deep plate that holds food

brave
not afraid to do something scary

a brave firefighter

bottle
something made of glass or plastic that holds liquids

box
something made of cardboard, wood or plastic that you can keep things in

bread
a food made from flour and baked in an oven

bottom¹
the part of your body that you sit on

boy
a child who is not a girl

break (broke, broken)
make something split into pieces or stop working

bottom²
the lowest part of something

The kitten is at the bottom of the stairs.

branch
part of a tree that grows from the trunk

breakfast
the first meal of the day

breakfast foods

a b c d e f g h i j k l m n o p q r s t u v w x y z

breathe

suck air through your nose or mouth and send it out again

Divers carry air to breathe underwater.

brush

something you use to tidy your hair, to clean your teeth or for painting

building

a place with walls and a roof

This building has ten floors.

bridge

something built over a road, river or railroad tracks so that people can get across

bucket

something you use to hold or carry things, such as sand or water

bump

knock into something or someone by mistake

Mr. Bun bumped into a dog.

bright

If a color or light is bright, it is strong and easy to see.

a bright yellow car

bug

an insect or other very small animal

burger

a round, flat piece of meat that you usually eat on a bun

bring (brought, brought)

take someone or something with you

Jack brought his letter to mail.

build (built, built)

make something by putting parts together

Billy is building a pyramid.

burn (burned, burned)

1. ruin or hurt something or someone with fire or heat

Dad burned the burgers.

2. be on fire

a b c d e f g h i j k l m n o p q r s t u v w x y z

bus
a big thing on wheels that can carry a lot of people

butter
a yellow food made from milk

café
a place with tables and chairs where you can buy and eat snacks and drinks

bush
a big plant with lots of branches. Bushes are smaller than trees.

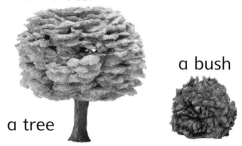

a tree   a bush

butterfly
an insect with four large wings

cage
a box or room with bars, for an animal

busy
If you are busy, you have lots of things to do.

Mr. Bun is busy in the kitchen.

button
a small, round thing that you use to fasten clothes

cake
a sweet, soft food that is baked in an oven

butcher
someone who sells meat

buy (bought, bought)
pay money for something so that you can have it

calf
a young cow

a cow and a calf

a **b c** d e f g h i j k l m n o p q r s t u v w x y z

call

1. shout to someone or a pet so that they come to you

Come here!

2. give someone or something a name

camel

a large animal with one or two humps

camera

something you use to take photographs

camp

live in a tent for a short time

candle

a lump of wax with a string through the middle

cap

a soft hat with a round part at the front that shades your eyes

car

a big thing that people drive. It has four wheels and goes on roads.

card

something that you send to people at special times

carpet

a thick cover that is attached to the floor

This room has blue carpet.

carrot

a long, orange vegetable

carry

hold something and take it with you

Aggie is carrying some flowers.

castle

a big, strong building with high, stone walls

a b c d e f g h i j k l m n o p q r s t u v w x y z

cat
a furry animal with a long tail

cave
a big hole in a mountain or cliff, or under the ground

There's a bear in this cave.

chair
a seat with a back, made for one person to sit on

catch (caught, caught)
1. get a hold of something that is moving

Jack caught the ball.

2. get on a bus, train or plane

CD (short for compact disc)
a round piece of plastic with music or information stored on it

chalk
soft white or colored sticks that you can use for writing and drawing

caterpillar
a small, long animal that will turn into a butterfly or moth

center
the middle part of something

The fruit is in the center of the table.

chase
run after a person or animal to try to catch them

Jack and Polly are chasing the dogs.

cauliflower
a big vegetable with green leaves and a white middle

cereal
a kind of food that you eat with milk for breakfast

cheap
not costing much

Everything in this shop is very cheap.

a b c d e f g h i j k l m n o p q r s t u v w x y z

cheese
a food made from milk

chicken (also called a hen)
1. a bird that farmers keep

2. a kind of meat that comes from a chicken

choose (chose, chosen)
pick the things that you want

Billy can't decide which to choose.

chef
someone who cooks the food in a restaurant

child (children)
a young boy or girl

city
a very big town where a lot of people live and work

cherry
a small, round fruit with a pit in the middle

chin
the part of your face below your mouth

class
a group of people who learn together

chick
a very young chicken or other bird

a hen with five chicks

chocolate
a sweet food used to make cakes, candy and drinks

classroom
a special room where people have lessons

a b c d e f g h i j k l m n o p q r s t u v w x y z

clean¹
take the dirt off something

clean²
not dirty

The boy in the middle is the only one with clean clothes.

climb
move up or down something high or tall

The firefighter is climbing up the ladder.

clock
something that shows the time

close¹ (say "kloze")
shut something

Danny is going to close the door.

close² (say "klose")
near

Bill and Ben are standing close together.

clothes
things that you wear

cloud
white or gray shapes that you see floating in the sky

clown
someone who wears funny clothes and does tricks to make people laugh

coat
something you wear to keep you warm when you go outside

coffee
a hot, brown drink made from roasted coffee beans

coin
a small, round piece of metal money

Pete has two coins in his hand.

a b c d e f g h i j k l m n o p q r s t u v w x y z

cold[1]
an illness that makes you cough and sneeze a lot

Helen has a bad cold.

cold[2]
not hot or warm

Sam is wearing gloves because it is cold.

color
Red, green, yellow and blue are all colors.

comb
something made from metal or plastic that you use to tidy your hair

come (came, come)
1. move towards somebody or something

The clown comes into the house.

2. arrive
What time does the bus come?

computer
a machine that stores words, pictures and numbers and can send messages

cook
heat food to make it ready to eat

Dad is cooking pancakes.

copy
do the same as someone

Sally is copying Polly.

country[1]
a part of the world with its own name, people and laws

This map shows the countries of Africa.

country[2]
the land outside towns and cities

cow
a big farm animal. Most milk comes from cows.

crash
hit something suddenly and make a loud noise

This car has crashed into a tree.

a b c d e f g h i j k l m n o p q r s t u v w x y z

C

crawl *to* cycle

crawl
move on your hands and knees

crayon
a colored pencil or a pencil made from wax

creep (crept, crept)
move very quietly and slowly

crocodile
a big animal with sharp teeth and a long tail

cross[1]
a mark made of two lines

cross[2]
go from one side to the other

Danny is crossing the road.

crown
a special gold or silver hat that a king or queen wears

cry
let tears fall from your eyes. You cry when you are hurt or unhappy.

cucumber
a long, green vegetable that you eat in salads

cup
something that you drink from. A cup usually has a handle.

cut (cut, cut)
use a knife or scissors to divide something into pieces

cycle
ride a bicycle

Sara cycles to school.

a b c d e f g h i j k l m n o p q r s t u v w x y z

Dd dance *to* desk

dance
move your body to music

Steff and Laura are dancing.

day
1. the time when it is light outside

2. the 24 hours between one midnight and the next

delicious
very nice to eat or drink

Jack's sandwich is delicious.
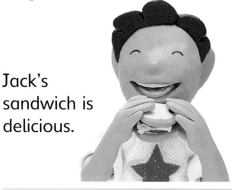

dangerous
If something is dangerous, it may kill or hurt you.

Some snakes are dangerous.

dear
a word that you use at the beginning of a letter

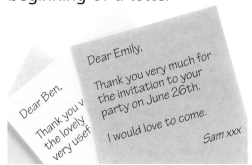

Dear Ben,
Thank you v
the lovely
very usef

Dear Emily,
Thank you very much for the invitation to your party on June 26th.
I would love to come.
Sam xxx

dentist
someone who takes care of your teeth

dark
1. When it is dark, there is no light.

2. not pale or light

dark blue paint

deep
going down a long way

The digger is digging a deep hole.

desert
very dry land where not many plants can grow

date
the day and month when something happens

January

Monday	Tuesday	Wednesday	Thursday	Friday	Saturday	Sunday
		1	2	3	4	5
6	7	8	9	10	11	12
13	14	15	16	17	18	19
20	21	22	23	24	25	26
27	28	29	30	31		

What's the date today?

deer
a big animal that can move quickly. Male deer have big horns called antlers.

desk
a kind of table that you sit at to read, write or use a computer

a b c **d** e f g h i j k l m n o p q r s t u v w x y z

dictionary

a book of words. It tells you what words mean and how to spell them.

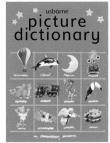

a picture dictionary

dig (dug, dug)

make a hole in the ground

dirty

covered with mud, food or other stains

die

When someone or something dies, they stop living.

I forgot to water my plant and it died.

digger

a big machine that can dig holes and move earth

disappear

If something disappears, you cannot see it any more.

Polly's dog has disappeared.

different

not the same

The twins are wearing different colors.

dinner

a name for the biggest meal of the day

dive

jump into water with your hands and head first

difficult

not easy to do

It's difficult to take care of two babies at the same time.

dinosaur

an animal that lived a long time ago. Some dinosaurs were enormous.

diver

someone who wears special clothes to swim underwater

a b c d e f g h i j k l m n o p q r s t u v w x y z

do *to* dream

do (did, done)

1. make something

Jenny is doing
a jigsaw puzzle.

2. finish
something

dolphin

a smart animal that lives
in the sea. Dolphins are
not fish.

dragon

a monster in stories that has
a long tail and wings and
breathes out fire

doctor

someone who helps sick
people get better

donkey

an animal that looks like a
small horse with long ears

draw (drew, drawn)

make a picture with a pen,
pencil or crayons

dog

an animal that people keep
as a pet or to do work

door

something you use to get
into a room, building, car
or cupboard

drawing

a picture someone has made
with a pen, pencil or crayons

doll

a toy that looks like a small
person

down

from a higher place to a
lower one

This arrow
points
down.

dream

a story that you see and
hear while you are sleeping

a b c d e f g h i j k l m n o p q r s t u v w x y z

dress[1]
something that girls and women wear

Anya is wearing a red dress with white flowers.

dress[2]
put on clothes

drink (drank, drunk)
swallow water or another liquid because you are thirsty

drive (drove, driven)
make a car, bus or other machine go somewhere

Mick is driving a dump truck.

drop[1]
a tiny bit of water or another liquid

drop[2]
let something fall

Ellie has dropped her cake.

drum
a musical instrument that you hit with sticks or your hands

dry[1]
take the water off or out of something or someone

Anna is drying herself with a towel.

dry[2]
not wet or damp

These clothes are dry.

duck
a bird that lives near water and can swim

duckling
a young duck

This duck has three ducklings.

dull
1. not very bright

a dull color

2. not very interesting

a dull story

a b c **d** e f g h i j k l m n o p q r s t u v w x y z

eagle

a big bird with sharp claws and a curved beak

ear

a part of your body that you use to hear

early

If you are early, you arrive sooner than someone expected.

Lucy arrived at the party early.

Earth

1. the planet that we live on

2. earth

the stuff that plants grow in

easy

not hard or difficult to do

$$1 + 1 = ?$$

an easy sum

eat (ate, eaten)

put food in your mouth and chew and swallow it

edge

the part along the side or end of something

The crayon is on the edge of the table.

egg

a smooth, oval thing that may contain a baby bird, fish or insect.
We often eat cooked hens' eggs.

elbow

one of the two bony parts in the middle of your arms that make them bend

electricity

something that makes lights, televisions, computers and other things work

Electricity comes through wires to make a television work.

elephant

a very big, gray animal, with a long nose called a trunk

e-mail

a message that you can send from one computer to another

Polly is sending an e-mail to her friend.

a b c d **e** f g h i j k l m n o p q r s t u v w x y z

empty
with nothing in it

This jar is empty.

envelope
a paper cover for a letter or card

evening
the part of the day between the afternoon and night

The sun sets in the evening.

end
the last part of something

the end of a TV film

equal
If things are equal, they are the same.

Sally and Amy have equal amounts of sand.

expensive
If something is expensive, it costs a lot of money.

Which toy is more expensive?

enjoy
If you enjoy something, you like doing it.

Molly enjoys singing.

escape
get away from somewhere

Jack's cat escaped from his arms and ran away.

explain
make something clear so other people will understand it

Mr. Levy is explaining how to do these sums.

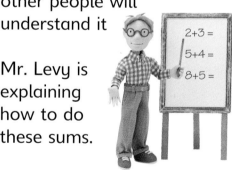

enormous
very big

Whales are enormous.

even
An even number is a number that you can divide by two.

The bunny is jumping on even numbers.

1 2 3 4 5 6 7

eye
a part of your body that you use to see

a b c d **e** f g h i j k l m n o p q r s t u v w x y z

face

the front part of your head

a happy face

fall (fell, fallen)

go down to the ground suddenly

The clown fell in a pink pie.

fast

If someone or something is fast, they move very quickly.

Eric can ski very fast.

facing

looking toward someone or something

These giraffes are facing each other.

far

a long way

The pet store isn't far from the butcher's store.

fat

with a big, round body

a fat cat

fact

something that is true

It's a fact that little babies sleep a lot.

farm

a place where a farmer keeps animals and grows food

feed (fed, fed)

give food to a person or animal

fairy

a tiny person, in stories, with wings

farmer

someone who has a farm

feel (felt, felt)

1. touch something to find out more about it

2. If you feel happy, for example, that is how you are at the time.

a b c d e **f** g h i j k l m n o p q r s t u v w x y z

fence

a kind of outdoor wall made from wood or wire

fill

put so much into something that there is no space for any more

Ivan has filled his wheelbarrow with sand.

fire

heat and bright light that comes from something that is burning

few

not many

Becky only has a few strawberries.

find (found, found)

see or get something that has been lost

Megan found the crayons.

fire engine

a kind of truck that carries all the things firefighters need to put out fires

field

a big piece of land where people grow plants or keep animals

finger

one of the five long, thin parts at the end of your hand

firefighter

someone whose job is to put out fires

fight (fought, fought)

When people fight, they try to hurt each other.

The children are fighting.

finish

come to the end of something

Danny has almost finished his juice.

first

before all the others

Jenny is first in the line.

a b c d e f g h i j k l m n o p q r s t u v w x y z

fish¹ (fish)

an animal that lives and breathes underwater. We eat some kinds of fish.

fish²

use a net or a rod to try to catch fish

fit¹ (fit, fit)

If clothes fit you, they are the right size.

Jenny's sweater doesn't fit. It's too big for her.

fit²

healthy and strong

Alice plays tennis to keep fit.

fix

repair something that is broken

Eve is fixing her doll.

flag

a piece of cloth with a special pattern on it. Each country has its own flag.

the French flag

flat

without any curves or bumps in it

Mr. Clack is sawing a flat piece of wood.

float

1. stay on the surface of water

2. stay up in the air

flood

a lot of water that covers ground which is usually dry

floor

the part of a room that you walk on

The floor is covered in toys and clothes.

flour

a powder usually made from wheat that you use to make bread and cakes

flower

a part of a plant. Flowers are often bright colors.

a b c d e **f** g h i j k l m n o p q r s t u v w x y z

fly[1]

a small insect with see-through wings

fly[2] **(flew, flown)**

move through the air

Birds can fly.

foal

a young horse

a foal   a horse

fold

bend one part of something over another part

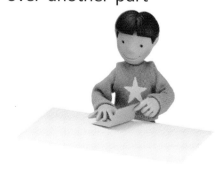

food

what you eat to stay healthy

foot (feet)

a part of your body at the end of your leg

forest

a place where a lot of trees grow close together

forget (forgot, forgotten)

If you forget something, you don't remember it.

Jan has forgotten which way to go.

fork

something that you use to eat with. It has three or four points.

fox

a wild animal that looks a little like a dog. Foxes have long, bushy tails.

free

1. If something is free, you don't have to pay for it.

2. allowed to go where you want or do what you want

freeze (froze, frozen)

become very cold

When water freezes, it turns into ice.

a b c d e **f** g h i j k l m n o p q r s t u v w x y z

freezer
a machine that keeps food very cold so that it does not go bad

fresh
1. If food is fresh, it has just been made or picked and is not bad.

Mrs. Martin sells fresh fruit.

2. If air is fresh, it is clean.

friend
someone that you like and who likes you

Ellie's friends are coming to her party.

friendly
If you are friendly, you like to meet other people and are kind to them.

Marco is very friendly.

frog
a small animal that lives near water. It has big back legs for jumping.

front
the part that comes first or that you see first

front door of a car

fruit
something such as an apple or orange that grows on a bush or tree

fry
cook something in oil or butter

Dad is frying some eggs.

full
If something is full, it cannot hold any more.

Greg's cart is full of groceries.

fun
If something is fun, you enjoy it and it makes you happy.

Ben and Suki are having fun on the merry-go-round.

funny
If something is funny, it makes you laugh.

Polly and Jack are laughing at a funny joke.

fur
the soft hair that covers some animals

a cat with soft, white fur

a b c d e **f** g h i j k l m n o p q r s t u v w x y z

game

something that you play, such as basketball or cards. Games often have rules.

gentle

If you are gentle, you are careful, quiet and kind.

Pip is a gentle dog.

gift

something special that you give to someone or that they give to you

garden

a piece of land near a house, where people grow vegetables and flowers

gerbil

a small, furry animal with long legs. Some people keep gerbils as pets.

giraffe

an African animal that has a very long neck and legs

gas

something that is not solid or liquid, and is very light and invisible like air

This balloon is filled with a gas called helium.

ghost

a person who has died that some people think they can see

girl

a child who is not a boy

gate

a kind of door in a fence, wall or hedge

giant

a very tall person, in a story

give (gave, given)

let someone have something to keep

Ethan is giving Jenny four wagons for her train.

a b c d e f **g** h i j k l m n o p q r s t u v w x y z

glad *to* goose

glad
pleased and happy

Sally is very glad to see her friend.

glass
1. something hard and clear that windows are made from

2. a kind of cup that is made from glass

glasses
something that you can wear on your face to help you see better

glove
something that you wear on your hand to keep it warm

glue
a thick liquid that you use to stick things together

Danny is gluing down paper shapes with glue.

go (went, been)
move or travel from one place to another

These cars are going onto the ship.

goal
when you kick, hit or throw a ball into a net, in games such as soccer

GOAL!

goat
a farm animal with a short tail

gold
a yellow metal that is very expensive

good (better, best)
1. If something is good, you like it.

2. done well

good work

3+3=6 ✓
2+5=7 ✓
8-6=2 ✓
4+1=5 ✓

3. not naughty

goodbye
a word you say when you go away or someone goes away from you

Goodbye!

goose (geese)
a large bird with a long neck

a b c d e f **g** h i j k l m n o p q r s t u v w x y z

33

grape

a small, soft purple or green fruit that grows in bunches

a bunch of grapes

ground

what you walk on outside

Polly is looking at some ants on the ground.

guess

try to think of an answer to something that you do not know

Can you guess what's in the box?

grapefruit

a large, round fruit with a thick yellow or pink skin

group

a number of people or things that are together

a group of children

guest

someone who comes to visit or stay for a short time

Ellie is welcoming her guests to her party.

grass

a plant with thin, green leaves. Grass grows in fields and yards.

grow (grew, grown)

get bigger

My plant grew very fast.

guinea pig

a small, furry animal that doesn't have a tail

great

1. big or important

2. very good

We had a great day at the beach.

grown-up

someone who is not a child

Grown-ups are always talking.

guitar

a musical instrument with strings

a b c d e f **g** h i j k l m n o p q r s t u v w x y z

Hh hair *to* hard

hair
the stuff that grows on your head

Rosie has long hair. Katie has curly hair.

hammer
a tool that you use for knocking nails into something

hang (hung, hung)
put something on a hook, nail or knob

Jack is hanging his coat on a hook.

hairbrush
something you use to brush your hair

hamster
a small, furry animal with a short tail

happen
take place

What is happening in this picture?

half (halves)
one of two pieces of something that are exactly the same size

Each mouse has half of the sandwich.

hand
a part of your body at the end of your arm

happy
If you are happy, you feel pleased about something and not sad.

Sally is feeling very happy today.

hamburger
a round, flat piece of meat that you usually eat on a bun

handle
something you use to hold or move something

hard
1. solid and not soft
2. not easy; difficult

It's hard to put up a tent on hard ground.

a b c d e f g h i j k l m n o p q r s t u v w x y z

35

hat

something that you wear on your head

hear (heard, heard)

take in sounds through your ears

Woof woof!

Jack can hear a dog barking.

height

how tall someone or something is

Dad is checking Milo's height on the chart.

hate

If you hate something, you do not like it at all.

Maddy hates spiders.

heart

1. the thing that pushes blood around your body

My heart is beating fast.

2. a shape

helicopter

a machine that flies. It has blades on top that spin around very fast.

have (had, had)

1. If you have something, it is with you.

Julia has some new red shoes.

2. feel or suffer

Helen has a cold.

heat

make something hot

Yvonne is heating coffee in the microwave.

hello

a word you say when you meet someone

Hello!

head

the part of your body that has your eyes, mouth and ears in it

heavy

hard to lift, push or pull; not light

Thomas and Jack are trying to move a heavy package.

helmet

a hard hat that stops you from hurting your head

Grace wears a helmet for skateboarding.

a b c d e f g **h** i j k l m n o p q r s t u v w x y z

help
do something useful for someone

Jack is helping his dad with the cooking.

hen (also called a chicken)
a bird that farmers keep

hide (hid, hidden)
1. go to a place where no one can see you

The clown is hiding from Annie.

2. put something in a place where no one can find it

high
1. a long way from the ground

The balloon is high in the sky.

2. going up a long way

highchair
a special chair for babies and small children

hill
a high piece of land. Hills are not as tall as mountains.

hippopotamus
(also called a hippo)
a very big animal with short legs and thick skin

hit (hit, hit)
push or knock someone or something very hard

Alice is hitting the ball with her racket.

hold (held, held)
1. have something in your arms or hands

2. have room for something

How many does this hold?

hole
a gap or hollow space in something

There is a hole in this sweater.

home
the place where you live

honey
a sweet, sticky liquid that bees make

a b c d e f g **h** i j k l m n o p q r s t u v w x y z

hop
jump on one leg

hotdog
a special kind of sausage that you eat in a long, soft bun, with mustard

hug
put your arms around someone or something and hold them tightly

horse
a big animal with four legs and a long tail. People ride horses.

hotel
a big building with a lot of bedrooms. You can pay to stay there.

hungry
If you are hungry, you want to eat something.

Oliver is very hungry.

hospital
a building where you go when you are sick or hurt. Doctors and nurses work at hospitals.

hour
an amount of time. There are 60 mintues in an hour and 24 hours in a day.

On a clock, the little hand shows the hours.

hurry
do something fast

Jack and Polly are hurrying to catch a bus.

hot
very warm; not cold

Don't touch the hot saucepans!

house
a building that people live in

hurt (hurt, hurt)
If something hurts, you feel pain there.

Ross is crying because his tummy hurts.

a b c d e f g **h** i j k l m n o p q r s t u v w x y z

ice
water that has frozen solid

ice cubes

ice cream
a very cold, sweet food made from cream or milk

idea
something new that you think of

I know, let's go to the park!

Andy has an idea.

insect
a small animal with six legs

inside
in something

This kitten is inside a flowerpot.

in a building; indoors

instead
in place of something

Let's have iced tea instead of juice this afternoon.

Internet
millions of computers all over the world linked together. You can use the Internet to find out things.

Polly is using the Internet.

invitation
something that you give someone to ask them to do something with you

Imogen invites Bob to a
Jungle Party
on Saturday, April 6th
at Oxten Community Center
at 2:00
RSVP

invite
ask someone to come somewhere or do something

Can you come to my party?

iron
something you use to make your clothes smooth

island
a piece of land with water all around it

itch
If your skin itches, you want to scratch it.

George's ear itches.

a b c d e f g h i j k l m n o p q r s t u v w x y z

jacket
a short coat

Kathy is wearing a yellow jacket.

jar
something that you keep things in. Jars are usually made of glass.

jeans
pants made from a strong material called denim

jigsaw puzzle
a picture cut into pieces. You put the pieces together to make the picture again.

job
1. what someone does to earn money

Aggie has a job as a gardener.

2. something that needs to be done

join
1. become part of a club or group

2. attach two things together

Ethan's going to join the wagons to the train.

joke
something you say to make people laugh

What flowers are between your nose and chin?

Tulips!

journey
If you go on a journey, you travel from one place to another.

a train journey

juggle
keep two or more things in the air by throwing and catching them, one after the other

juice
liquid that comes from fruit or vegetables

jump
use your legs to push yourself suddenly into the air

jungle
a place in a hot country where many trees and plants grow and many animals live

a b c d e f g h i j k l m n o p q r s t u v w x y z

kangaroo
a large animal that moves around by jumping

keep (kept, kept)
1. have something and not give it away

Sam keeps his things on a shelf.

2. make something stay the same

key
something you use to unlock a door or to start a car

kick
hit something with your foot

kid
1. a child

2. a young goat

a goat and a kid

kill
make something die

Someone has killed my plant.

kind[1]
a type or sort

There are lots of different kinds of fruit.

kind[2]
If you are kind, you help other people.

Mr. Dot is kind. He does all his neighbor's shopping.

king
a man who rules a country. Kings come from royal families. They are not chosen.

Adam is dressed up as a king.

kiss
touch someone with your lips

kitchen
a room where you make meals

kite
a toy that flies in the wind on the end of a long string

a b c d e f g h i j **k** l m n o p q r s t u v w x y z

k kitten *to* know

Ll ladder *to* lake

kitten
a young cat

This kitten is playing with a ball of yarn.

knight
a soldier who lived a long time ago. Knights wore armor and rode horses.

ladder
something you can use to climb up to high places

knee
the bony part in the middle of your leg that makes it bend

knock
hit something hard

Pip knocked the chair over.

lady
a woman

These ladies are talking.

kneel (knelt, knelt)
get down on your knees

knot
a place where something, such as string, is tied

ladybug
a small red or yellow insect with black spots

knife (knives)
something you use to cut things. It has a long, sharp edge and a handle.

know (knew, known)
1. If you know someone, you have met them before.

These children know each other.

2. have something in your mind

lake
a big area of water with land around it

a b c d e f g h i j k l m n o p q r s t u v w x y z

lamb

a young sheep

a sheep and a lamb

lamp

something that makes light

land

the parts of the Earth that are not covered by water

This map shows the land in brown.

language

the words that people use to speak and write

Alex and Polly are speaking different languages.

large

If someone or something is large, they are big.

Becky is standing under a large tree.

last

1. at the end

The black dog is last.

2. the time before

late

1. after the right time

The bus is late again.

2. near the end of something

laugh

make sounds that show that you think something is funny

lazy

If a person or an animal is lazy, they do not want to do anything.

a lazy cat

lead (led, led)

go in front to show the way

This duck is leading her ducklings.

leaf (leaves)

one of the thin, flat parts of a plant or tree

lean (leaned, leaned)

bend to one side

the Leaning Tower of Pisa

a b c d e f g h i j k l m n o p q r s t u v w x y z

learn *to* lick

learn (learned, learned)
get to know and understand something you did not know before

Steve is learning to play the guitar.

lemon
a yellow fruit with a thick skin

let (let, let)
If someone lets you do something, they say that you can do it.

Mr. Dot let Jack mail his letter.

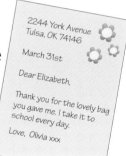

leave (left, left)
1. go away from a place

Mr. Bun is leaving.

2. let something stay where it is

I left my bag at home.

length
how long something is

Use a ruler to measure the length of the paper.

letter
1. something like A, B or Z that you use to make words

2. a message that you write on paper

2244 York Avenue
Tulsa, OK 74146

March 31st

Dear Elizabeth,

Thank you for the lovely bag you gave me. I take it to school every day.

Love, Olivia xxx

left
on the side opposite the right side

Lisa is holding the crayon in her left hand.

less
not as much

Ethan has less ice cream than Olivia.

lettuce
a vegetable with big leaves that you eat in salads

leg
a part of your body that you use for standing and walking

Tamsin wears tights on her legs.

lesson
the time when someone teaches you something

2 + 4 = 6

lick
move your tongue across something

a b c d e f g h i j k l m n o p q r s t u v w x y z

lid

the top of something like a box or jar

lid

lie¹ (lay, lain)

rest with your body flat on something like a bed

lie²

say something that is not true

Is she in there?

No!

life (lives)

the time when someone or something is alive

Granny and Granddad have had long and happy lives.

lift

pick something up

The clown is lifting a tree out of his bag.

light¹

1. Light comes from the Sun and from lamps. It lets you see.

2. something that gives light, such as a lamp

light²

1. easy to lift, push or pull; not heavy

2. If a color is light, it is pale and not dark.

light pink

like¹

If you like something or someone, you think they are nice.

Becky likes strawberries.

like²

If someone is like another person, they are the same in some way.

Sarah looks a lot like her brother.

line

1. a long, thin mark

2. a group of people or things in a row

a line of soccer players

lion

a big, wild animal with light brown fur

lip

the edge of your mouth

lip

a b c d e f g h i j k l m n o p q r s t u v w x y z

l

list *to* lunch

list

words that someone has written down one after the other

long

1. If something is long, one of its ends is far from the other.

A giraffe has a long neck.

2. lasting a lot of time

loud

If someone or something is loud, they make a lot of noise.

Steve's guitar is very loud.

live

1. If you live in a place, that is where your home is.

2. If someone or something lives, they are alive.

look

use your eyes to see something

Polly is looking at the clown.

love

like someone or something very much

Beth loves taking a bath.

lock

something that keeps things like doors and boxes shut. You need a key to open a lock.

a lock ——

lose (lost, lost)

1. If you lose something, you can't find it.

2. If you lose a game, you don't win it.

Simon and Ian lost.

low

not far from the ground

This bird is flying very low.

log

a big piece of wood that has been cut from a tree

lot

a large amount or number

a lot of bears

lunch

the meal you eat in the middle of the day

Sally is eating pizza for lunch.

a b c d e f g h i j k l m n o p q r s t u v w x y z

Mm machine *to* meal

machine
something with moving parts that work together to do a job

a sewing machine

man (men)
a grown-up who is not a woman

Our teacher is a man.

match¹
1. a game that two teams play against each other

a tennis match

2. a small stick that makes fire when you rub its tip against its box

magic
1. In stories, people use magic to make impossible things happen.

2. clever tricks that look impossible

The clown is doing some magic.

many (more, most)
a large number; a lot of

There are many bees on this flower.

match²
If things match, they are like each other in some way.

These socks match.

These socks don't match.

main
the biggest or most important

the main entrance of the museum

map
a drawing that shows where places are. Maps show roads, rivers and buildings.

matter
If something matters, it is important to you.

Winning really matters to Neil and his team.

make (made, made)
1. put something together

Ethan is making potato people.

2. If you make something happen, it happens because of something you do.

market
a place where you can buy things. Markets are often outdoors.

meal
the food that you eat at special times of the day. Breakfast, lunch and dinner are meals.

a b c d e f g h i j k l m n o p q r s t u v w x y z

m

mean *to* milk

mean (meant, meant)
1. If you say what something means, you explain it.

This means that two groups of two equals four.

2 x 2 = 4

2. plan to do something

measure
find out how big or heavy something is

meat
a kind of food that comes from animals

medicine
a liquid or pill that you take when you are sick to make you better

meet (met, met)
If you meet someone, you both go to the same place at the same time.

Polly and Lisa met at the fruit stand.

mend
repair something that is broken

Robert is mending his shirt.

mess
untidy and sometimes dirty

What a mess!

message
words that you send or leave for someone when you can't speak to them

Mom!
Paula called about tomorrow.
Call her back.

metal
hard stuff that comes out of the ground. Gold, silver, iron and copper are metals.

This bucket is made of metal.

microwave
a small oven that cooks or heats up food very fast

middle
the place that is the same distance away from all the sides of something

This bear is in the middle of the grass.

milk
a white liquid that you can drink. Milk usually comes from cows.

a b c d e f g h i j k l **m** n o p q r s t u v w x y z

mind *to* more

mind

be worried or unhappy about something

I don't mind spiders.

mistake

If you make a mistake, you do something wrong.

I made a spelling mistake.

choc~~k~~olate
business
animal
mixture
dinosaur

monkey

an animal with a long tail and long arms and legs

minute

an amount of time. There are 60 seconds in a minute and 60 minutes in an hour.

It's a few minutes past nine.

mix

put things together to make one thing

Oliver is mixing flour, sugar, eggs, butter and raisins to make a cake.

month

a part of the year that lasts about 4 weeks. There are 12 months in a year.

| January |
| February |
| March |
| April |
| May |
| June |
| July |
| August |
| September |
| October |
| November |
| December |

mirror

a special piece of glass that you can see yourself in

model

a small copy of something

Billy is playing with his model ship.

Moon

the big, bright thing that you often see in the sky at night

miss

1. feel unhappy because someone is not with you

Liddy misses her mom.

2. not catch a bus or train

money

coins and bills that you use to buy things

more

a bigger number, amount or size

Sally   Amy

Sally has more sand than Amy.

a b c d e f g h i j k l m n o p q r s t u v w x y z

49

morning
the part of the day before 12 o'clock (noon)

mountain
a very high piece of land. Mountains are taller than hills.

much (more, most)
a big amount

Mrs. Moon doesn't have much to carry.

most
the biggest number or amount

Which caterpillar has the most black stripes?

mouse
1. (plural: mice) a small, furry animal with a long tail

2. something you use to move things around on a computer screen

mud
wet earth

Sally is covered in mud.

moth
an insect with four large wings

mouth
the part of your face that you use to eat and talk

mushroom
a kind of plant that is the shape of a small umbrella. You can eat some kinds of mushrooms.

motorcycle
a big, heavy bicycle with an engine

move
1. go from one place to another
2. take something from one place to another

The crane is moving the box.

music
the sounds that you make when you sing or play a musical instrument

a b c d e f g h i j k l m n o p q r s t u v w x y z

Nn

nail *to* nest

n

nail

1. a pointed thing that you use to join pieces of wood together

2. one of the hard parts at the end of your fingers and toes

name

what you call a person or thing

What's your toy's name?

Her name is Tabby.

narrow

If something is narrow, its sides or edges are not far apart.

The gap is too narrow for the kitten to get through.

nature

everything in the world, such as plants and animals, not made by people

naughty

If you are naughty, you do things that you are not meant to do.

Naughty Pip has stolen a piece of Jack's cake.

near

not far away; close

The school is near the river.

neck

the part of your body that joins your head to your shoulders

A giraffe has a very long neck.

necklace

something pretty that you wear around your neck

need

If you need something, you must have it.

Sam needs sleep.

needle

1. a thin, pointed piece of metal that you use for sewing

2. a long metal or plastic stick that you use for knitting

neighbor

someone who lives near you

The people who live in these two houses are neighbors.

nest

a home made by birds and some other animals. Birds lay their eggs in nests.

a b c d e f g h i j k l m **n** o p q r s t u v w x y z

net[1]

1. a kind of bag that you use to catch fish and other animals

2. the thing you hit balls over in games such as tennis

Net[2]

a short name for the Internet

Polly is using the Net.

never

not at any time

The grumpy mailman never smiles.

new

1. just made, bought or born

Julia has new shoes.

2. different

a new school

news

information about things that have happened in your life or in the world

I've lost my cat!

Mrs. Beef has some sad news.

newspaper

big sheets of paper with stories and pictures about the news

next

1. the one after this

2. nearest to; beside

The red car is next to a yellow car.

nice

If you think something is nice, you like it.

Danny has made a nice picture.

night

the time when it is dark outside and people sleep

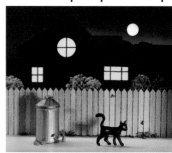

nod

move your head up and down

The dog is nodding.

noise

a sound that someone or something makes

WAAAH!

The baby is making lots of noise.

noisy

very loud

The boys are being very noisy.

a b c d e f g h i j k l m n o p q r s t u v w x y z

nose
the part of your face that you use to smell and breathe

note
1. a sound that you make when you sing or play music

a high note

2. a short message that you write

Remember to feed the cat!

notebook
a book with clean pages for you to write on

notice
see something and pay attention to it

Annie hasn't noticed the clown.

now
at this time

The clown takes a pie out of his bag...

...now he trips.

number
a word or sign that shows how many

I   7   88   1,200
three   twenty-two
one hundred

nurse
someone who takes care of people who are sick or hurt

nut
something with a hard shell. Many kinds of nuts are good to eat.

ocean
a very large sea

o'clock
a word you use when you say what time it is

It's seven o'clock.

octopus
a sea animal with eight long arms

odd
1. An odd number is a number that you can't divide by two.

The bunny is jumping on odd numbers.

I   2   3   4   5

2. strange or unusual

a b c d e f g h i j k l m **n** o p q r s t u v w x y z

often

If you do something often, you do it a lot.

Mr. Dot and Jack often do the shopping.

oil

a thick liquid. Some oil is used to make machines work or to make heat. Some oil from plants is used for cooking.

cooking oil

old

1. If someone or something is old, they have lived for a long time.

2. made or bought some time ago

an old shoe

once

1. only one time

We went up in a balloon once.

2. after; as soon as

You can watch TV once you've done your homework.

onion

a round vegetable with papery skin and a strong smell and taste

only

and no more; just

Becky only has two strawberries.

open¹

1. move something such as a door so that you can go through it

2. take the lid off something

Mrs. Dot is opening the box.

open²

If something is open, you can go through it or into it.

The pet store is open all day.

opposite¹

The opposite of something is the thing that is the most different from it.

Big is the opposite of small.

opposite²

If two things or people are opposite each other, they are facing each other.

Becky is sitting opposite the teddy bear.

orange

1. a round, juicy fruit with a thick skin

2. a color

other

1. different

Do you have any other toys?

No, just cars.

2. one of two
Where's your other shoe?

a b c d e f g h i j k l m n o p q r s t u v w x y z

outside

1. not inside a building

Let's go outside!

2. not in something

The monkey is outside the box.

over

1. on top of

The bird is flying over the tree.

2. above or across
3. finished
4. down

owl

a bird with big eyes. Owls catch small animals at night.

own

If you own something, it is yours.

Mrs. Bird owns a pet store.

page

a piece of paper attached inside a book

Turn the page.

paint¹

a special liquid that you use to put color on things

jugs of paint

paint²

1. use a brush and paints to make a picture

2. put paint on something to change its color

pair

the name for two things that go together

a pair of socks

palace

a very large house where kings, queens, princes and princesses live

pale

If a color is pale, it is very light.

pale blue

pale green

pale yellow

paper

1. something that you write, draw and paint on

2. short for newspaper

parachute

a large piece of cloth that can carry people safely to the ground from a plane

a b c d e f g h i j k l m o p q r s t u v w x y z

parent

a mother or father

Mr. and
Mrs. Dot
are Polly
and Jack's
parents.

park[1]

a big piece of land where
people can walk and play

park[2]

leave a car somewhere

Jan and Jo are going to
park in the parking lot.

parrot

a bird with bright feathers
and a curved
beak

part

something that belongs to
something bigger

A wheel is part of a car.

party

when a group of friends
meet to eat, drink and have
fun together

a costume
party

pass

1. go past someone
or something

passing the bank

2. give something to someone
when they can't reach it

3. do well in a test or exam

past[1] .

the time that has gone

This is how some people
dressed in the past.

past[2]

by or beside

The children and dogs are
running past the pet store.

path

a small road for people to
walk or ride on

paw

an animal's foot

a tiger's paw

pay

give someone money for
something

Ethan is
paying for
an apple.

a b c d e f g h i j k l m n o p q r s t u v w x y z

pea *to* person

pea
a very small, green, round vegetable

peach
a soft, round fruit with a furry skin

peak
1. the very top of a mountain

2. the round, front part of a cap

peak

peanut
a small, oval nut. Peanuts are often roasted before you eat them.

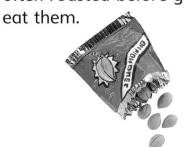

pear
a juicy green or yellow fruit

pebble
a smooth, round stone. You find pebbles on beaches.

pen
a metal or plastic thing that you use to write or draw in ink

pencil
a long, thin piece of wood with a black stick in the middle that you use for writing and drawing

penguin
a black and white bird that lives in cold places

people
men, women and children

There are seven people here.

pepper
1. a black or gray powder you can put on food to add flavor.

2. a type of vegetable

person
a man, woman or child

This person is a builder.

a b c d e f g h i j k l m n o p q r s t u v w x y z

57

pet
an animal that you keep at home

phone (short for telephone)
something you use to talk to someone in another place

photograph
a picture that you take with a camera

Polly is looking at photographs.

piano
a musical instrument with black and white keys that you tap with your fingers

pick
1. choose something

2. take fruit or flowers from a tree or plant

picnic
a meal that you take to eat outdoors

picture
a painting, drawing or photograph

piece
a part of something

pillow
something that you rest your head on when you are lying in bed

pilot
someone who flies a plane

Jim wants to be a pilot when he grows up.

pineapple
a large yellow or brown fruit, with pointed leaves at the top

pizza
a flat, round piece of bread with tomatoes, cheese and other food on top

a b c d e f g h i j k l m n o **p** q r s t u v w x y z

place *to* pocket

place

somewhere such as a building, country or town. It can be very big or small.

a good place for a snack

plan¹

a map of a building or a place

plan²

decide how to do something

Mrs. Dot is planning a party.

plane (short for airplane)

a big machine that flies

planet

an enormous, round thing that goes around the Sun. The Earth is a planet.

plant

a living thing that grows in soil or in water. Trees and flowers are plants.

plate

a round, flat thing that you put food on

play

1. do something for fun

2. use a musical instrument to make music

3. take part in a sport

playground

a place where you can play outdoors

please

a word that you say when you ask for something in a polite way

Could I please have some more strawberries?

plum

a small, soft fruit with red, purple or yellow skin

pocket

a small bag that is part of your clothes. You can keep things in your pockets.

Renata is putting her hands in her pockets.

a b c d e f g h i j k l m n o **p** q r s t u v w x y z

p

poem *to* press

poem
a piece of writing. Poems usually have short lines and may have words that rhyme.

My Cat

My cat is sitting in the sun,
While I am having lots of fun.
My cat is sleeping in the house,
And dreaming that she's caught a mouse.

by Polly Dot

point¹
1. the sharp end of something

the point of a pencil

2. part of the score in a game

I have three points now.

point²
use your finger to show where something is

Polly is pointing to Jack's nose.

police
The police are people whose job is to stop people from breaking the law.

police car
a special car that the police use for their work

pond
a small area of water

pony
a small horse

pool
a place where people go to swim or play in the water

poor
1. If you are poor, you don't have much money.

2. a word you use when you feel sorry for someone

Poor Ross, his tummy hurts.

potato
a white, red or brown vegetable that grows under the ground

present
something special that you give to someone or that they give to you

press
push something

Danny is pressing down the blue paper to make the sea.

a b c d e f g h i j k l m n o p q r s t u v w x y z

pretend
act as if something is true when it is not

pretending to be asleep

pretty
nice to look at

Anya is wearing a pretty red dress.

price
how much money something costs

2 for the price of 1

prince
the son of a king or queen

princess
the daughter of a king or queen or the wife of a prince

prize
something that you win when you do well

promise
say that you will really do something

I promise I'll take you to the park.

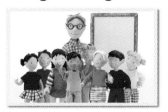

puddle
a small pool of water on the ground that you see after it has been raining

pull
move someone or something toward you

Thomas   Jack

Jack is pulling the big package.

pumpkin
a very big, round fruit with a hard orange or yellow skin

pupil
someone who is learning something, usually in a school

a photo of Mr. Levy and some of his pupils

puppet
a kind of doll that you make move

a b c d e f g h i j k l m n o p q r s t u v w x y z

Qq

puppy
a young dog

a puppy and a dog

push
move someone or something away from you

Thomas is pushing the big package.

Thomas   Jack

put (put, put)
move something to a place

Oliver is putting a bottle of green paint on the table.

puzzle
a game that you have to think about very carefully

quack
When a duck quacks, it opens its beak and makes a loud sound.

Quack! Quack!

quarter
one of four pieces of something that are the same size

a quarter

queen
a woman who rules a country. Queens are not chosen.

Joy is dressed up as a queen.

question
what you say or write when you want to find out something

What's your name?

quick
1. If someone or something is quick, they move very fast.

2. lasting only a short time

quiet
not making much noise

You need to be very quiet to creep up on someone.

quite
1. fairly or rather

I'm quite tired.

2. completely

Mr. Bun hasn't quite finished all his baking.

quiz
a kind of game where you have to answer questions

Animal Quiz
1) Which is the biggest animal in the world?
2) What kind of animal is a toucan?
3) Where in the world can you see ostriches and cheetahs?
4) What kind of animal was a Triceratops?

a b c d e f g h i j k l m n o **p q** r s t u v w x y z

rabbit
a furry animal with long ears and a short tail

rainbow
a curved band of different colors that you sometimes see in the sky

reach
1. stretch out your hand to touch something

The firefighter is reaching out to rescue the cat.

2. arrive at a place

race
a competition to find out who is the fastest

raisin
a small, dried grape that you can eat as a snack or in muffins

read (read, read)
look at words and understand what they mean

radio
a machine that plays music and programs that you can listen to

raspberry
a small, soft, red fruit

ready
If you are ready, you can do something immediately.

These children are ready to swim.

rain
If it rains, drops of water fall down from the sky.

rat
a small animal with a long tail and sharp teeth

real
1. not a copy

Is that fruit real or plastic?

2. true

I like real adventure stories.

a b c d e f g h i j k l m n o p q **r** s t u v w x y z

recorder *to* ring

recorder
a musical instrument that you blow into

rescue
help someone or something escape from danger

rich
If you are rich, you have a lot of money.

a rich popstar

refrigerator
a kind of metal cupboard that keeps food cold

rhinoceros
(also called a rhino)
a very big animal with thick skin and horns on its nose

ride (rode, ridden)
sit on a bicycle or horse and move along

remember
bring something into your mind again

Fiona can remember the order of the colors of the rainbow.

red, orange, yellow, green, blue, indigo, violet

ribbon
a long, thin piece of cloth that you tie around things

Becky has green ribbons in her hair.

right
1. without any mistakes in it

That's the right answer.

2. the side opposite the left side

The puppet is on Greta's right hand.

reply
give an answer

Do you want to go to the park?

Yes please.

Minnie is replying to her dad's question.

rice
a food that comes from a kind of grass plant. You cook and eat grains of rice.

ring¹
1. something pretty that you wear around your finger

2. a circle with a hole in the middle

a b c d e f g h i j k l m n o p q r s t u v w x y z

ring² (rang, rung)

When a bell or telephone rings, it makes a loud noise.

rrring!

The phone's ringing.

ripe

If fruit is ripe, it is soft and ready to eat.

river

a wide line of water that flows across land to the sea

These houses are near the river.

road

a hard piece of ground that goes from one place to another

robot

a machine that can do some of the things that people do

a toy robot

rock

1. a very big stone

2. a kind of music with a strong beat

Steve likes to play rock music.

rocket

a machine that takes astronauts into space. Rockets travel very fast.

a toy rocket

roof

the part of a building that keeps the rain out

roof

room

1. a space inside a building with walls around it

This plan shows six rooms.

2. space

Is there any room for me?

rope

something made of lots of strong threads twisted together. You can use a rope for pulling heavy things.

rose

a flower with a prickly stem. Many roses smell nice.

round

shaped like a circle or ball

Drums are usually round.

a b c d e f g h i j k l m n o p q **r** s t u v w x y z

rug

something that covers part of a floor

ruler

a flat piece of plastic, wood or metal that you use to measure things and draw straight lines.

run (ran, run)

move quickly using your legs

rush

do something quickly; hurry

Jack, Polly and the dogs are rushing past the post office.

sad

not happy

saddle

a seat for a rider on a horse

 —— saddle

safe

1. If you are safe, you are not in danger.
2. If something is safe, it can't hurt you.

a safe place to cross

sailor

someone who works on a ship

salad

a mixture of uncooked food, such as lettuce and tomatoes

salami

a kind of big sausage with a strong flavor. You usually eat thin slices of salami.

salt

a white powder that you put on food or use in cooking to add flavor

same

If two things or people are the same, they are just like each other.

The twins always wear the same clothes.

a b c d e f g h i j k l m n o p q r s t u v w x y z

sand *to* scooter

sand
a powder made of tiny pieces of rock and shell. It covers some beaches and deserts.

sandal
a kind of shoe that you wear when it is hot

sandwich
two pieces of bread with another kind
of food
between
them

saucer
a small plate that you put under a cup

a cup and saucer

sausage
something that you eat made from chopped meat put into a special skin

save
1. rescue someone or something from danger

2. keep money
to spend later

Jack saves coins in
this cow money bank.

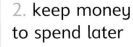

saw
a tool that you use to cut wood

say (said, said)
speak words

There was an old woman who lived in a shoe...

scarf
a long thing that you wear around your neck to keep warm

school
a place where children go to learn

scissors
something you use to cut paper or cloth

scooter
a small machine that you can push along with one foot

a b c d e f g h i j k l m n o p q r s t u v w x y z

sea

a very large area of salty water

seal

an animal with smooth fur that lives in the sea and on land

search

look carefully for something

Annie, Megan and Tim are searching for their friend.

seat

a place where you can sit

secret

something that only a few people know

Amy is telling Anna a secret.

see (saw, seen)

1. use your eyes to look at something

Can you see the clown?

2. meet someone

I'll see you on Monday.

sell (sold, sold)

let someone have something if they give you money

Mrs. Hussain is selling Ethan an apple.

send (sent, sent)

make something or someone go somewhere

Jack is sending a letter to his friend.

sentence

a group of words that makes sense. A sentence starts with a capital letter and ends with a period.

My dad likes apples.

a sentence

sew (sewed, sewn)

connect pieces of cloth together using a needle and thread

shadow

a dark shape that is made by something getting in the way of light

shake (shook, shaken)

move something up and down or from side to side

Anton loves to shake his rattle.

a b c d e f g h i j k l m n o p q r **s** t u v w x y z

shallow

not going down very far;
not very deep

The wading pool is shallow.

shampoo

a liquid that you use when
you wash your hair

share

let someone have a part of
something or use something
with you

Bill is sharing
his cherries
with Ben.

shark

a big fish with sharp teeth

sharp

If something is sharp, it has
a very thin edge or a point
that can cut or prick you.

a sharp pencil

sheep (sheep)

a farm animal with a wooly
coat. Most wool comes from
sheep.

sheet

1. a big piece of cloth that
you put on a bed

2. a flat piece of paper, glass
or plastic

shelf (shelves)

a long, flat piece of wood,
metal or plastic that is
attached to a wall

shell

1. the hard cover around
some sea animals and snails

2. the hard part around eggs
and nuts

ship

a very big boat that carries
people and things over the
sea

shirt

something that you wear on
the top part of your body.
A shirt often
has buttons
down
the front.

shoe

something you wear to cover
your foot

a b c d e f g h i j k l m n o p q r s t u v w x y z

short

1. not very long

Maisie has short hair.

2. not tall

Minnie is short for her age.

shorts

pants with short legs

shoulder

a part of your body between your neck and your arm

Jack's shoulder

shout

talk very loudly

COME BACK PIP!

show (showed, shown)

1. let someone see something

Jack is showing Thomas his hands.

2. explain how to do something by doing it yourself

shower

1. something you use to wash yourself

2. a short fall of rain

shrink (shrank, shrunk)

get smaller

This pink sweater shrank in the wash.

shut (shut, shut)

move a door or cover to block a space or opening; close

Danny is shutting the door of the playhouse.

side

1. the edge of something

2. a flat surface of something

A piece of paper has two sides.

3. a team

sign[1]

1. words or pictures that tell you what to do

a road sign

2. a shape that means something

@ is the sign for "at".

sign[2]

write your name on something

Sign here please.

since

from that time

They've been waiting for the bus since 2:30.

a b c d e f g h i j k l m n o p q r **s** t u v w x y z

sing (sang, sung)

use your voice to make music

sink¹

something that you wash things in. Sinks have faucets and a plug.

sink² (sank, sunk)

go downward underwater

sit (sat, sat)

put your bottom on something and rest

size

how big or small something is

skate

move smoothly on ice wearing special boots called skates

ski

travel on snow wearing two long things called skis on your feet

skin

1. the cover of your body

Babies have smooth skin.

2. the outside layer of a fruit or vegetable

skirt

something that girls and women wear

sky

the space above the ground where you can see clouds, stars and planes

sleep (slept, slept)

close your eyes and rest your whole body, usually at night

sleeve

a part of a shirt, top, coat, or sweater that covers your arms

a b c d e f g h i j k l m n o p q r s t u v w x y z

slice
a piece of food that has been cut from a larger piece

slide¹
something you can play on in a playground

slide² (slid, slid)
move smoothly over or down something

slip
slide and fall over

slipper
a soft shoe that you wear indoors

slow
If someone or something is slow, they take a long time to go somewhere or do something; not fast.

a slow train

slowly
If you do something slowly, it takes a long time.

Sally is riding slowly so that she doesn't spill any sand.

slug
a small, soft animal with no legs, like a snail without a shell

small
not big, large or tall; little

Asha is a small child.

smell (smelled, smelled)
1. use your nose to sense something

2. If something smells, you can sense it with your nose.

Your cat smells horrible!

smile
turn up the corners of your mouth to show that you are happy

smooth
If something is smooth, it does not have bumps or lumps in it.

The roller is making the road smooth.

a b c d e f g h i j k l m n o p q r **s** t u v w x y z

snail

a small, soft animal with no legs and a shell on its back

snake

a long, thin animal with no legs. Some snakes have a poisonous bite.

snow

small, white pieces of ice that fall from the sky when it is very cold

soap

something you use to wash yourself

soccer

a game where two teams try to kick a ball into a net

sock

something you wear on your foot under your shoe

sofa

a long, soft chair for two or more people

soft

not hard or firm

This cat has soft fur.

soil

the earth that plants grow in

soldier

someone whose job is to fight

song

a piece of music with words that you sing

I love you baby... boom ba, boom ba

Natalie is singing a song.

soon

happening not long from now

It will soon be 2 o'clock.

a b c d e f g h i j k l m n o p q r s t u v w x y z

sort

a kind or type

different sorts of food

spacecraft

something that travels into space from the Earth

spell² (spelled, spelled)

write or say the letters of a word in the right order

sound

something that you hear

Parrots make a squawking sound.

speak (spoke, spoken)

say something

spend (spent, spent)

use money to buy things

Danny is thinking about how to spend his money.

soup

a liquid food made from meat or vegetables and water

special

1. important or better than usual

2. made for a particular job

Electricians need special tools.

spider

a small animal with eight legs

space

1. an empty place or area

2. everything outside the Earth, including the stars and planets

spell¹

In stories, a spell is special words or a recipe that makes things change or happen.

spill (spilled, spilled)

let liquid fall out of a container by mistake

a b c d e f g h i j k l m n o p q r **s** t u v w x y z

spinach *to* star

spinach
a vegetable with dark green leaves

sport
a kind of game that you play to get exercise and have fun

stairs
a group of steps inside a building

splash
throw liquid around

spot¹
a small, round mark

a dog with black spots

stamp
a small piece of paper with a picture on it that shows you have paid to mail something

sponge
something you can use for cleaning things or soaking up liquid

spot²
notice something

Can you spot a clown in this picture?

stand (stood, stood)
be upright on your feet

spoon
something you use for stirring things and for eating

squirrel
a small animal with a big, furry tail

star
1. a little bright light you can see in the sky at night

2. a shape with points

3. a famous person

a movie star

a b c d e f g h i j k l m n o p q r s t u v w x y z

75

start

do the first part of something; begin

The birds are starting to eat the seeds.

station

a place where people get on or off trains

stay

1. not leave a place

The cows stay in the field all day.

2. live somewhere for a short time

steep

If a hill is steep, it slopes a lot and is hard to climb.

stick¹

a long, thin piece of wood

stick² (stuck, stuck)

use glue to join something onto something else.

still¹

If someone or something is still, they are not moving at all.

Milo is standing very still.

still²

If something is still happening or is still there, it has not stopped or gone.

Oliver ate one apple...

...but he still has some left.

sting (stung, stung)

If an animal or plant stings you, it pricks you and leaves some poison in your body.

Flora is afraid the bee will sting her.

stir

move something around with a spoon or stick

stone

a small rock

stool

a seat without a back

a b c d e f g h i j k l m n o p q r s t u v w x y z

stop

1. not move any more

Jan and Jo stopped at the gate to take a ticket.

2. not happen any more

strawberry

a soft, red fruit with tiny seeds on its skin

study[1]

a room for reading, writing or working on a computer

storm

a strong wind with lots of rain or snow

street

a road in a town or city which usually has buildings on both sides

study[2]

learn about something

story

words which tell you about something that has happened. A story can be true or made up.

The Magic Ring

Once upon a time there was a very kind old lady who lived in a cottage in the forest with 100 cats. Her name was Mrs. Fussalot and she had five granddaughters named Milly, Molly, Maggie, Maddy and Mandy. One day Mrs.

string

very thin rope that you use to tie things together

suddenly

If something happens suddenly, it happens quickly and when you don't expect it.

Suddenly she dropped the vase.

straight

If something is straight, it does not bend or curve.

Leslie has straight hair.

strong

1. able to lift heavy things

2. If something is strong, it does not break easily.

3. with a lot of flavor

strong coffee

sugar

sweet, white or brown stuff that you can put in drinks or in food

a b c d e f g h i j k l m n o p q r s t u v w x y z

suitcase

a kind of strong bag for carrying clothes and other things

sunglasses

something that you can wear on your face to shade your eyes from the Sun

swan

a big white or black bird with a long neck

sum

a math question using numbers

$$8 + 2 =$$
$$4 - 2 =$$
$$10 \times 4 =$$

supermarket

a big store that sells food and other things

sweep (swept ,swept)

use a broom to clean the floor or ground

Sun

the very large, bright thing that you see in the sky in the daytime

sure

If you are sure about something, you know it is true or right.

Dad isn't sure if they've got everything on the list.

sweet

1. lovely; cute

a sweet kitten

2. kind

3. If food is sweet, it has the taste of sugar.

sunflower

a very tall flower with yellow petals

surprise

something that you do not expect

BOO!

It was a surprise when the clown jumped out.

swim (swam, swum)

move through water using your arms and legs

a b c d e f g h i j k l m n o p q r s t u v w x y z

swimming pool
a place made for people to swim in

swimsuit
special clothes that you wear for swimming

swing[1]
something you can sit on in a playground to go backward and forward

swing[2] (swung, swung)
move backward and forward on something that is hanging

table
a piece of furniture with a flat top and legs

tail
the part at the end of some animals' bodies

tail

take (took, taken)
1. move or carry something

Amy is taking sand to the sandpit.

2. steal something

talk
speak to people

tall
If someone or something is tall, their head or top is high above the ground.

taste
put food or drink in your mouth to find out what it's like

taxi
a car that you can pay to ride in

tea
a drink made from hot water and dried leaves from a tea plant

a tea bag

a b c d e f g h i j k l m n o p q r s t u v w x y z

teacher
someone whose job is to teach other people

team
a group of people who work or play sports together

teddy bear
a soft, furry toy that looks like a bear

telephone
(also called a phone) something you use to talk to someone in another place

television
(also called a TV) something that shows moving pictures and sends out sounds

tell (told, told)
1. talk to someone about something

Mrs. Beef is telling them about her cat.

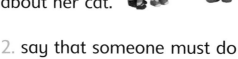

2. say that someone must do something

tent
a kind of small house made from strong cloth that you can sleep in outside

thank
tell someone that you are pleased with something they have done or given you

Polly is thanking Marco for the present.

thin
1. not wide; narrow

2. not weighing much; not fat

a thin cat

thing
anything you can see, touch, do or think about

There are lots of things on the table, but Tina still has a few things to do.

think (thought, thought)
1. use your mind

2. believe something

Maddy thinks spiders are scary.

thirsty
If you are thirsty, you want to drink something.

a b c d e f g h i j k l m n o p q r s t u v w x y z

through
from one side to the other

Mr. Bun went out through the door.

throw (threw, thrown)
make something move through the air

Anna is going to throw the ball.

thumb
the shortest of your five fingers, at the side of your hand

ticket
a small piece of paper that shows you have paid for something

tie
hold things together with a string, rope or ribbon

Someone has tied the ribbons together.

tiger
a big, wild animal with orange fur and black stripes

time
1. a moment shown on a clock or watch

2. how long something takes to happen

tiny
very small

a small cat   a tiny cat

tip
the very end part of something

This fox's tail has a white tip.

toast
a piece of bread which has been cooked until it turns brown

toddler
a young child who is just beginning to walk

toe
one of the five parts on the end of your foot

toe

a b c d e f g h i j k l m n o p q r s t u v w x y z

together

with another person or thing

Jenny and Ethan are playing together.

tonight

the night or evening of this day

I'm going to a party tonight.

top

1. the highest part of something

The kitten is on the top of the desk.

2. something that you wear on the upper part of your body

toilet

a special bowl with a seat where you go to the bathroom

tooth (teeth)

one of the hard white things inside your mouth that you use for biting and chewing

touch

1. feel something with part of your body

2. If things touch, they are so close there is no space between them.

Please do not touch!

tomato

a soft, juicy red fruit that you eat in salads

toothbrush

a brush that you use for cleaning your teeth

towel

a big piece of thick, soft cloth that you use to dry yourself

tongue

the long, soft part inside your mouth that you use for tasting, eating and talking

toothpaste

a thick liquid that you put on a toothbrush to clean your teeth

town

a place with lots of roads and buildings where many people live and work

a b c d e f g h i j k l m n o p q r s t u v w x y z

toy *to* twin

toy
something that you play with

tractor
a big thing with large back wheels. Farmers use tractors to pull other machines or heavy loads.

train
a very big thing that can carry a lot of people along on rails

tree
a very large plant with leaves, branches and a trunk

truck
a big thing with wheels that carries things from one place to another

true
1. correct or right

TRUE OR FALSE?
A. An aardvark is a plant.
B. Penguins can't fly.
C. Tadpoles turn into butterflies.

2. If a story is true, it really happened.

try
1. work hard to do something you want to do

They are trying to move the package.

2. test something

T-shirt
something with short sleeves that you wear on the top part of your body

turkey
1. a big bird that farmers keep

2. a kind of meat that comes from a turkey

turn
1. go in a different direction

They are going to turn left.

2. move around

TV
(short for television) something that shows moving pictures and sends out sounds

twin
Twins are two children who have the same mother and were born on the same day. Some twins look alike.

a b c d e f g h i j k l m n o p q r s t u v w x y z

ugly
not pretty to look at

undress
take your clothes off

upside down
with the part that is usually at the top at the bottom

umbrella
something you hold over your head to keep the rain off

unhappy
sad or upset

use
do a job with something

Mr. Clack is using a saw.

under
If something is under something else, it is lower than it.

The kitten is under the wooden boards.

upright
standing straight

useful
If something is useful, it helps you do something.

A wheelbarrow is useful for moving things.

understand
(understood, understood)
know what something means or how it works

Can you understand what Ben is saying?

Ben want dwink!

upset
not happy; angry

Mrs. Beef is upset because she has lost her cat.

usually
If something usually happens, it almost always happens.

Sara usually cycles to school.

a b c d e f g h i j k l m n o p q r s t u v w x y z

Vv vacuum cleaner *to* voice

Ww

wait *to* wake

vacuum cleaner
a machine that you use to clean carpets

vase
something you can put flowers in

vegetable
a plant that you can eat

very
You use the word "very" before another word to make it stronger.

dirty   very dirty

view
what you can see from a particular place

visit
go to see someone or something for a short time

The children are going to visit the museum.

visitor
someone who goes to a place to see someone or something

Polly has some visitors.

voice
the sound you make when you talk, shout or sing

LAAAAA!

wait
stay in a place until something happens

waiter
a man who brings the food and drink in a café or restaurant

waitress
a woman who brings the food and drink in a café or restaurant

wake (woke, woken)
stop sleeping

a b c d e f g h i j k l m n o p q r s t u v w x y z

walk

put one foot in front of the other to move along

wall

1. one side of a room or building

2. something made of stone or brick that divides land

want

If you want something, you need it or would like it.

Jenny wants some more wagons for her train.

warm

1. fairly hot

a warm day

2. making you feel fairly hot

a warm coat

wash

use soap and water to make someone or something clean

washing machine

a machine that washes clothes

watch¹

a small clock that you wear cn your wrist

watch²

look at someone or something to see what happens

water

the clear liquid that falls as rain and comes out of faucets

Becky is playing in the water.

wave¹

a big hill of water in the sea

wave²

move your hand from side to side to say hello or goodbye

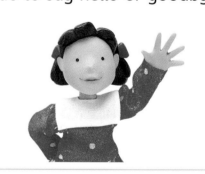

way

1. how you do something

2. how you get from one place to another

This is the way to the village.

a b c d e f g h i j k l m n o p q r s t u v w x y z

wear (wore, worn)

When you wear clothes, they cover your body.

Miriam is wearing a red suit.

weather

what it is like outside, for example windy, rainy, sunny or snowy

cold weather

web

1. a thin net that a spider makes to catch insects

2. Web the part of the Internet that you can use to find out information

week

A week is seven days. There are 52 weeks in a year.

well

1. If you are well, you are healthy.

2. If you do something well, you are good at it.

Sarah can read very well now.

wet

full of water or covered in water

whale

a very big animal that lives in the sea

wheel

a round thing that can turn around

while

at the same time as something else is happening

Jack ate a cake while no one was looking.

wide

measuring a lot from one side to the other; not narrow

This sofa is wide enough for three cats.

wild

not looked after by people; not tame

wild animals

win (won, won)

come first in a game, race or competition

The pink cake won first prize.

a b c d e f g h i j k l m n o p q r s t u v w x y z

wind

air that moves quickly

The wind blew Alison's hat off.

window

something in a wall or in a car that lets in light. There is usually glass in a window.

wish

something you want to happen very much

This fairy can give you three wishes.

witch

a woman in a story who can do magic spells

with

1. If you are with someone, you are together.

2. using
Draw with a pencil.

3. that has or who has

a bird with blue feet

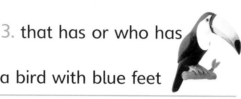

woman (women)

a grown-up who is not a man; a lady

wood

the hard part of a tree that can be burned or used to make things

a table made of wood

word

a group of sounds or letters that means something. You use words to speak and write.

a list of words

work

1. do a job or something that needs to be done

Mick works as a builder.

2. If something works, it does what it should do.

world

the planet that we live on

write (wrote, written)

use a pen or pencil to put letters or words on something

HARRY

Harry has written his name.

wrong

1. not correct or right

All these answers are wrong.

2 + 3 = 7 X
4 + 6 = 9 X
5 − 3 = 4 X

2. naughty or bad

a b c d e f g h i j k l m n o p q r s t u v w x y z

Xx *x to* xylophone

x

1. You write x after your name to send someone a kiss.

Lots of love from Kathy xxx

2. times or multiplied by

$$2 \times 2 = 4$$

Xmas

a short way of writing "Christmas"

Happy Xmas!

x-ray

a kind of photograph that shows the inside of someone's body

xylophone

a musical instrument with a row of wooden or metal bars. You play it by hitting the bars with special sticks.

Yy yawn *to* young

yawn

open your mouth and breathe in deeply because you are tired

year

A year is 12 months.

Freya is five years old. Annie is six years old.

yet

up to this time

Ben can't walk yet.

young

If someone or something is young, they have only lived a short time.

young children

Zz zebra *to* zoo

zebra

an animal that looks like a horse with black and white stripes

zero

the name for the number 0; nothing

$$5 - 5 = 0$$

Five take away five equals zero.

zipper

something that you use to fasten clothes and bags

zoo

a place where wild animals are kept so that people can go to see them

We saw a panda at the zoo.

a b c d e f g h i j k l m n o p q r s t u v w x y z

Colors

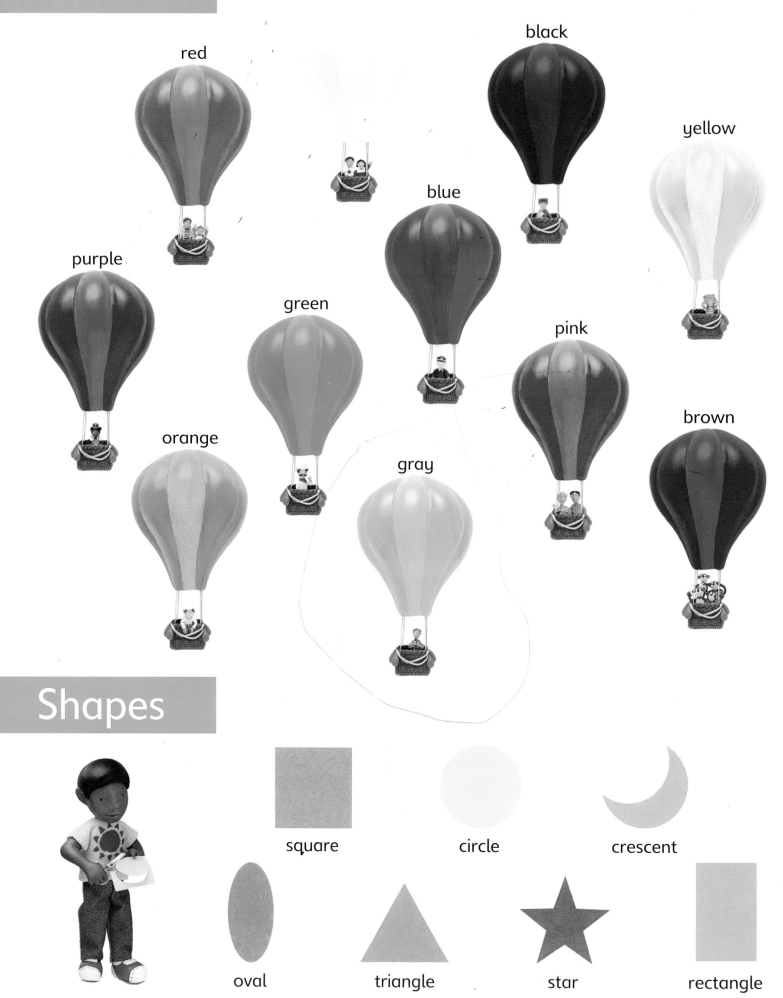

white

red

black

yellow

purple

blue

green

pink

orange

brown

gray

Shapes

square

circle

crescent

oval

triangle

star

rectangle

90

Numbers

first   second   third   fourth   fifth   sixth   seventh   eighth   ninth   tenth

1st   2nd   3rd   4th   5th   6th   7th   8th   9th   10th

1	one	
2	two	
3	three	
4	four	
5	five	
6	six	
7	seven	
8	eight	
9	nine	
10	ten	
11	eleven	
12	twelve	
13	thirteen	
14	fourteen	
15	fifteen	
16	sixteen	
17	seventeen	
18	eighteen	
19	nineteen	
20	twenty	

30	40	50	60	70	80	90	100	1000
thirty	forty	fifty	sixty	seventy	eighty	ninety	hundred	thousand

Days and months

Monday

Tuesday

Wednesday

Thursday

Friday

Saturday

Sunday

January

February

March

April

May

June

July

August

September

October

November

December

Polly's birthday is in January. When is your birthday?

92

Seasons

Spring

Summer

Fall

Winter

Family words

Polly is looking at some photographs of her family.

Polly and Jack are sister and brother.

Here are Polly's parents. She calls her mother "Mom" or "Mommy". She calls her father "Dad" or "Daddy".

Jack is his parents' son.

Polly is her parents' daughter.

Here are Polly and Jack with their grandparents. Polly calls her grandmother "Granny". She calls her grandfather "Granddad". What do you call yours?

Here's Daddy with his brother Howard.

Here's Jack when he was a baby.

Howard is Polly's uncle. His wife, Kathy, is Polly's aunt. Their little girl is Polly's cousin Aimee.

Polly and Jack are their parents' children. They are their grandparents' grandchildren. Polly is their granddaughter. Jack is their grandson.

Words we use a lot

a
about
above
across
again
all
almost
also
always
am
among
an
and
another
anybody
anyone
anything
anywhere
apart
are
around
as
at
away

be
because
but
by

can
can't
could
couldn't

each
every
everybody
everyone
everything
everywhere

for
from

get
got

he
he'd
he'll
her
here
hers
herself
he's
him
himself
his
how

I
I'd
if
I'll
I'm
in
into
is
isn't
it
its
it's
itself

just

may
me
might
mine
must
my
myself

no
nobody
none
no one

not
nothing
nowhere

of
off
on
or
our
ours
ourselves
out

she
she'd
she'll
she's
should
so
some
somebody
someone
something
sometimes
somewhere

than
that
the
their
theirs
them
themselves
then
there
these
they
they'd
they'll
they're
this
those
to
today

tomorrow
too

unless
until
up
upon
us

we
we'd
we'll
were
we're
what
when
where
which
who
whose
why
will
won't
would
wouldn't

yes
yesterday
you
you'd
you'll
your
you're
yours
yourself
yourselves

First published in 2002 by Usborne Publishing Ltd,
83-85 Saffron Hill, London EC1N 8RT, England.   www.usborne.com
Copyright © 2002 Usborne Publishing Ltd. First published in America 2002

Printed in Italy.